44822
√94

S0-BZJ-551

JE
F724b

Ben's Baby
Copyright © 1987 by Michael Foreman
Published in Great Britain by Andersen Press Ltd., London.
Printed in Italy. All rights reserved.
1  2  3  4  5  6  7  8  9  10
First American Edition

Library of Congress Cataloging-in-Publication Data
Foreman, Michael, 1938–
    Ben's baby / Michael Foreman. — 1st American ed.
        p.      cm.
    Summary: Ben asks his parents for a baby for his next birthday
and by the time it comes around he has a baby brother.
    ISBN 0-06-021843-6 : $       .
    ISBN 0-06-021844-4 (lib. bdg.) : $
    [1. Babies—Fiction.  2. Brothers—Fiction.]  I. Title.
PZ7.F7583Be  1987                                87-25943
[E]—dc19                                         CIP
                                                 AC

# Ben's Baby
## MICHAEL FOREMAN

OWENS TECHNICAL COLLEGE
LEARNING RESOURCES MEDIA CTR
CALLER 10,000 OREGON ROAD
TOLEDO, OHIO 43699

Harper & Row, Publishers

It was summer. It was Ben's birthday.

Ben's best present was a bike. He rode it to the park

and under the big trees by the river.

In the autumn he rode it through the swirling leaves while his mom and dad searched for chestnuts.

"What do you want for your next birthday, Ben?" asked his mom.
"A baby," said Ben. His dad laughed and stopped looking for
chestnuts.

At Christmas Ben got a soccer ball and a kite.

"Give me a hug, Ben," said his mom. "Can you feel that lump in my tummy?"
"Feels like another ball," said Ben.
"It's a baby," said his mom.

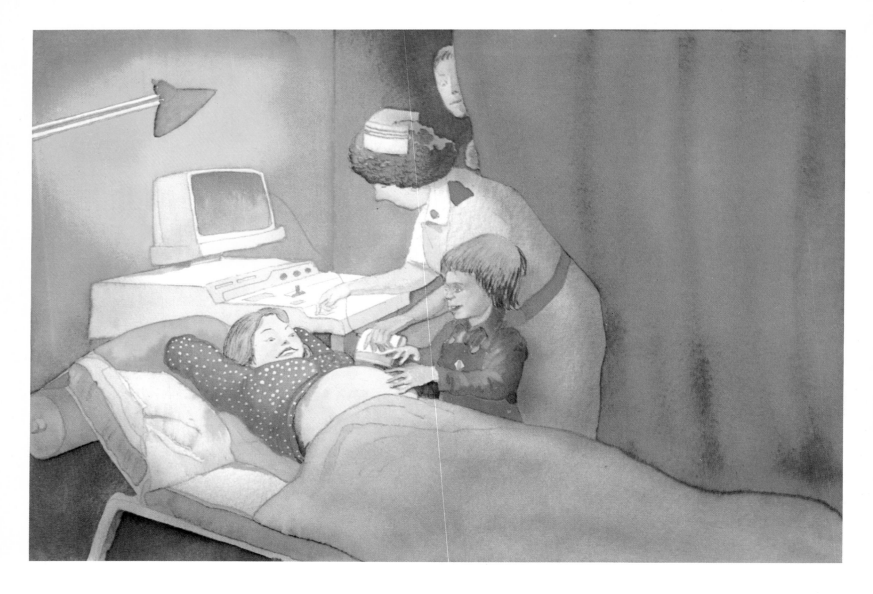

At the end of January, Ben and his mom and dad went to the hospital.

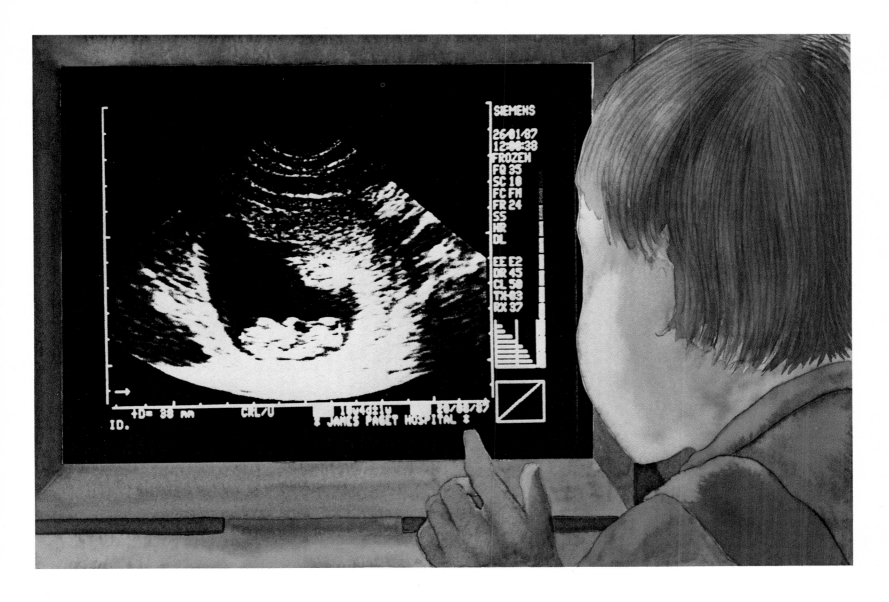

They saw a flickering picture on a screen.
"Is that my baby?" asked Ben. "Is it waving?"

Ben flew his kite by the sea, but the spring winds were too strong

and the kite crashed and broke.

His dad got him a new little folding kite that couldn't be broken and fixed the old one.

"Now we have two kites," said Ben. "One for me and one for my baby."

Then it was summer and Ben's birthday once more. There were
friends and balloons and a cake shaped like a robot.

There was a Punch-and-Judy show and ice cream, and Jill fell in the pond.

The next morning Ben's baby-sitter Maura made him breakfast

and took him to the museum. His mom and dad were at the hospital.

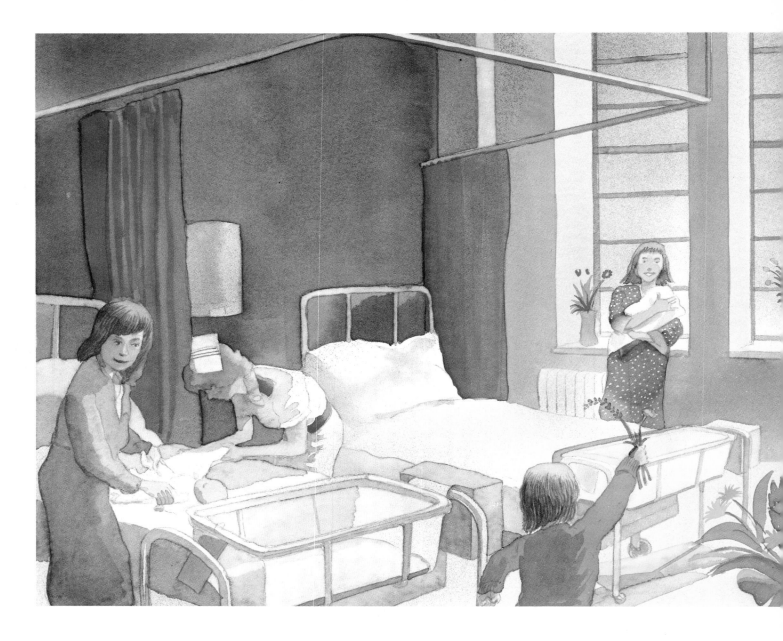

Later Ben's dad came home, and said, "Let's go and see your baby brother."
The hospital room was full of beds and crying babies.

 the corner by the big window was Ben's mom with a little bundle in her arms.
t's your baby, Ben," she said, and they all kissed the baby.

Two days later Ben and his dad brought Mom and the baby home.
The big chestnut trees were covered with blossoms like candles.

"Like birthday cakes for the new baby," said Ben.
Ben let the baby have his old crib and some of his old toys.

The next day was Sports Day at Ben's school, and the whole family was there.
Ben fell down in the first race and needed lots of bandages.
Mom and Dad gave him lots of hugs and kisses, too.

By now all his friends knew that Ben had a baby. He was very proud.

And they all walked home under the big trees by the river.